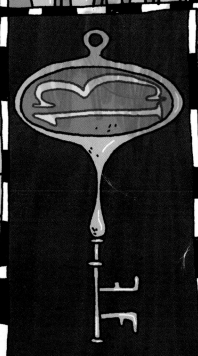

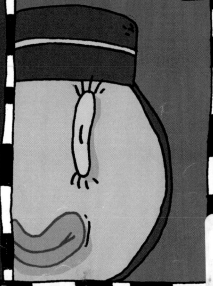

Boo!

Sean Diviny

BY **SEAN** "SCREAM INSIDE THE HOUSE" **DIVINY**
ILLUSTRATED BY **JOE** "THE REVENGE OF THE . . ." **ROCCO**

JOANNA COTLER GHOULS
A *Scream*print of HarperCollins*Publishers*

Halloween Motel
Text copyright © 2000 by Sean Diviny
Illustrations copyright © 2000 by Joe Rocco
Printed in the U.S.A. All rights reserved.
www.harperchildrens.com

Library of Congress Cataloging-in-Publication Data
Diviny, Sean.
    Halloween Motel / by Sean Diviny ; illustrated by Joe Rocco.
       p.   cm.
    Summary: When a family mistakenly checks into the wrong motel for
Halloween, they do not realize just how scary the other guests are.
    ISBN 0-06-028815-9 — ISBN 0-06-028816-7 (lib. bdg.)
    [1. Halloween—Fiction.   2. Hotels, motels, etc.—Fiction.   3. Stories
in rhyme.]   I. Rocco, Joe, ill.   II. Title.
PZ8.3.D6245 Hal   2000   99-89317
[E]—dc21   CIP
                                                            AC

Typography by Alicia "I Married a Monsterrobot" Mikles
1 2 3 4 5 6 7 8 9 10
❖
First Edition

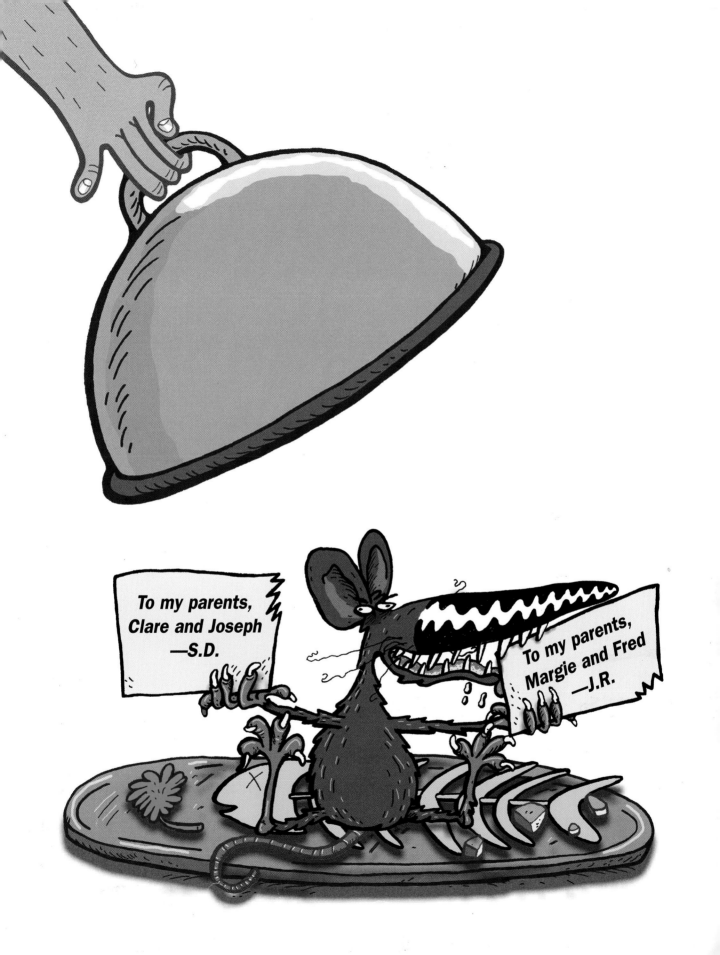

The broken buzzing neon sign had letters falling off.
The fog was thick and cold and damp. It gave my dad a cough!

The pool had something swimming in it—
really **long** and w**eird**!
A sign read, "Swim at your own risk.
The lifeguard **dis**appeared."

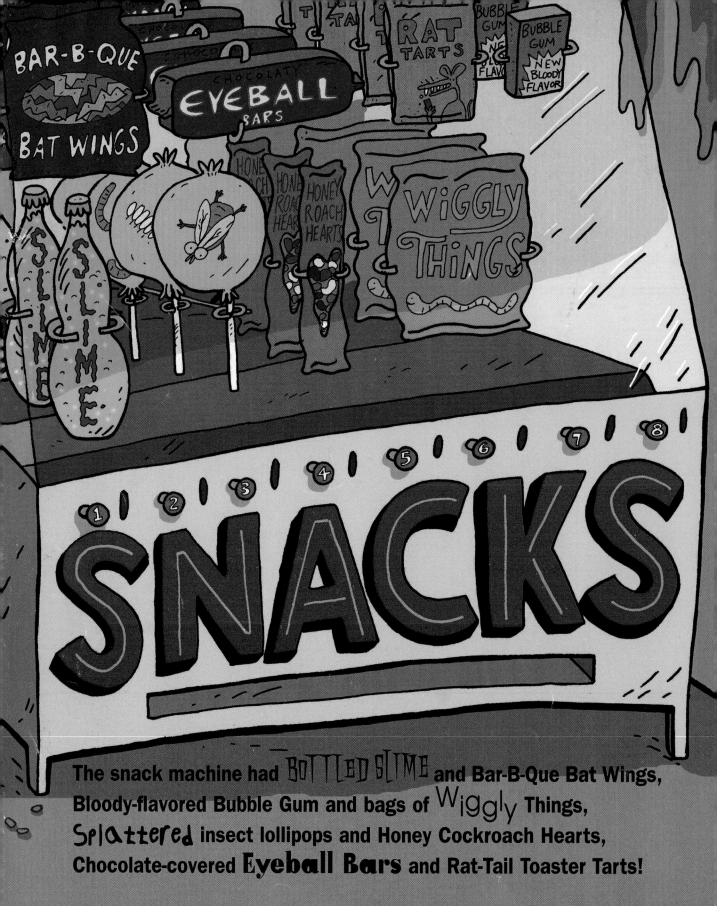

The snack machine had BOTTLED SLIME and Bar-B-Que Bat Wings,
Bloody-flavored Bubble Gum and bags of Wiggly Things,
Splattered insect lollipops and Honey Cockroach Hearts,
Chocolate-covered Eyeball Bars and Rat-Tail Toaster Tarts!

Halloween Motel. Oh, no!
They've got a vacancy.
Heed my warning. Don't you go!
Oh, turn around and flee!

The bed was kind of CREEPY with a tombstone at the head.
The phone looked like a skull and bone. I tried it. It was **dead!**
The TV turned on **by itself** and showed a horror flick.
The furniture had feet and claws that gave my mom a *kick!*

The bellman brought our luggage up.
His face was sort of hairy.
His eyes were *gooey yellow*,
and his BREATH was really scary!
My dad tipped him a quarter,
and he bared his teeth and *GROWLED*.
My mom gave him a dollar more,
and, joyfully, he howled!

"Now, let's see," my dad said
as he studied the brochure.
"Trick-or-treating starts at dusk.
Let's KNOCK on every door!"

My dad dressed up as Elvis. My mom was a baboon.
And I was Captain Muscle from that wrestling cartoon.
A **FULL MOON** rose behind us, and the motel seemed to glow.
"Time to trick-or-treat," said Mom. "C'mon, you two. Let's go!"

Vampires in
Room Seventeen
threw apples
that were
CHEWED!

Room Ten's *Ghostly Lady* only stared at us and *booed!*

The Aliens in Room Fourteen tossed out a **globe** and **map!**

The **Z**ombies in Room Six just growled, "We're *trying* to take a nap!"

"This is **FUN!**" said Mom. "The costumes really are uniQue. Let's come back again next year and stay here for a **W E E K** !"

Then FRANKIE STEIN lurched up to us and said, "Aha! It's true!
The guests have all complained about some weirdos, and they're you!"
"Now, wait a minute," said my dad. "I don't know what you mean.
You're called the *Halloween Motel,* but *don't like* Halloween?"

"**Halloween Motel**? Oh, no.
That's miles away from here.
We're the **Holiday** Motel,"
said Frankie with a **SNEER**.

We ran as *fast* as we could run and **JUMPED** into the car!
The monsters tried to chase us, but they didn't make it far.
We reached the right motel that night, and though we had some fun,
I still say Holiday Motel's the spOoky, scary one!

Holiday Motel. *That night!*
It really was the worst!
Stay there if you want a FRIGHT
OCTOBER 31st!